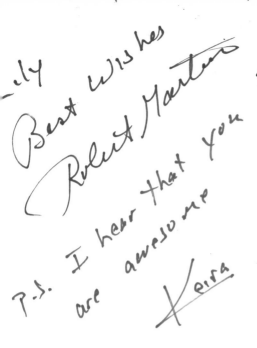

~ely

Best Wishes

Robert Martens

P.S. I hear that you
are awesome

Keira

The Keira and Papa Detective Agency

The Case of the
Missing Crown Jewels

Robert Martin
with Keira Martin Ely

DreamChaser Publishing

The Keira and Papa Detective Agency:
The Case of the Missing Crown Jewels
by Robert Martin with Keira Martin Ely
© 2015 Robert Martin
All rights reserved.

This is a work of fiction. Names, characters, places,
and incidents either are the product of the author's
imagination or are used fictitiously. Any resemblance
to actual persons living or dead, events or locales
is entirely coincidental.

Published by
DreamChaser Publishing LLC
RobertMartinAuthor.com

The Keira and Papa Detective Agency series is a
registered trademark of DreamChaser Publishing LLC

Illustrations: Tracy Rudd

Cover and Interior Design: Nick Zelinger, NZ Graphics
Book Consultant: Judith Briles, The Book Shepherd

ISBN: 978-0-9908317-0-9 Hardcover
ISBN: 978-0-9908317-1-6 Paperback
ISBN: 978-0-9908317-2-3 EBook

LCCN: 2015933544

Middle Grade Mystery

Printed in the United States of America

First Edition

Keira and Papa aren't the only grandchild and grandparent detectives.

What about you?

You may have one grandparent or as many as four. Either way, you're very lucky—grandparents are special friends. The mystery you are about to read will inspire you to form your own detective team with a grandparent. At the back of the book there are some suggestions to get you started.

Dynamic Duo

Grandparents are also a great resource, someone you can go to discuss many of the mysteries of everyday life. I've listed some examples of situations you might face that you would like to discuss with someone you can trust. Your grandparent is there to help, not judge.

Books in
The Keira and Papa Detective Agency series

The Case of the
Missing Crown Jewels

London

The Case of the
Vanishing Pharaoh

The Case of the
Mystical Bird

New York

The Case
of the
Golden Key

Panama City

The Case of the
Missing Transmitter

Cairo

Bangkok

Cast of Characters

Keira: a twelve-year-old, with a quick sense of humor, and a vivid imagination. She compliments her red hair and cool glasses with a multicolored wardrobe. She's somewhat shy.

Papa: a retired senior executive and secret agent for the CIA. Since retiring he has been bored.

Waffles: Keira's misbehaved puppy.

Kaya: Keira's American Girl™ Doll that is more than just a doll.

Commissioner Lamb: head of Scotland Yard (London police) and an old friend of Papa's. He has a close relationship with Keira. She calls him Uncle Commish.

Sir Hazledine: Secretary to the Queen of England. He is very formal and stiff. Doesn't like children or animals.

Director Shallow: Head of Security for the Tower of London, where the Crown Jewels are on display. Addicted to chocolate. He is nice looking but weighs 300 pounds. He is married to a former beauty queen.

Governor Foster: In charge of all aspects of the Tower of London. Comes from a well-established family. His father was an ambassador.

Prologue

Six months ago, my grandfather and I left his house at 5:30 A.M. We arrived at the beach in time to watch the sun poke a hole in the seam where the sky meets the sea. We took our usual position at a table and chairs on the beach club's stone patio next to the sand. No one else was there. All was normal, for the moment.

Papa, my grandfather, was on his laptop and I was scanning the horizon, when I noticed what looked like a head floating in the Long Island Sound. I leapt up and ran toward the water, shouting. "Papa, Papa, there is a dead body in the water!" He either didn't hear me or didn't believe me. It's not often that a corpse floats by. I was sure that this time it wasn't my wild imagination. It even wore a baseball cap. My pace slowed as I moved closer.

"Keira, stop! Don't move! Freeze, now!" Papa commanded.

"Let's get out of here," I screamed.

"Stay here. It will be OK," he replied with a much softer voice. He kissed my head, and then started toward the water's edge. He inched his way forward, his feet no match for the carpet of broken shells. "Ouch! Ouch!" he said with each step.

"Papa, stop! It's too dangerous," I yelled. I was sure that the floating body would leap out of the water and grab him. I sometimes let my imagination get the best of me.

As he bent over to pick it up, I wanted to run but I couldn't. It was like the sand had swallowed my legs. The fear worked its way up to my chest. I had to catch my breath. I had never seen a dead person before. I thought if I did, nightmares would follow forever. I couldn't look down into the water. I kept my eyes focused on Papa's face. Just as I was about to scream, I realized he was smiling, and saw what he was holding.

Papa put the ball between his legs and yanked with all his might to remove the baseball cap that was scrunched onto the ball. Although we laughed that it was only a hat stuck to a ball, I was still nervous. It had looked so real. I was thinking that at any moment an eye might pop out and it would turn into a gory Cyclops—my imagination's standard operating procedure when it comes to doing something. This is very different from "the anything is possible" of my daydreams.

Papa squeezed most of the seawater out of the hat, and tried to place it on my head.

"Papa, stop it! The hat is wet and yucky. How come grandfathers always like yucky things?" I didn't tell him that I was afraid there might be crabs and other scary creatures hidden inside.

He didn't reply. He curled his lower lip downward, pretending that I hurt his feelings. We both knew that he was kidding. It's part of the fun we have together.

Papa and I chased seagulls as we raced back up the beach to where we had been sitting. The seagulls took to the air just as we were inches from catching them. I arrived at the table before Papa. I could hear him muttering, "ouch! ouch!" the whole time as the clamshells played havoc with his feet.

"It's about time, slowpoke," I teased.

Papa laughed at my kidding then got serious. "Would you like to go home, Gumdrop?—that was quite a scare we had." Gumdrop is his special nickname for me.

Although I was still shaken, concerned that the Cyclops might still appear, I said, "No." I didn't want Papa to think I was a wimp. To convince him that I was OK, I said, "Hey, Papa, how come seagulls can fly?"

"I'm not sure. Let's look it up on my laptop."

Papa turned the computer on. However, the glare from the sun was too strong for us to see the screen clearly. I held my hand over my eyes but that didn't help much.

Papa put his hat on and said, "Keira, my hat's visor worked for me. I can see the screen now."

As Papa surfed the web searching for the answer, I slid the mysterious hat onto my head. I shivered. My imagination was up to its old tricks—I was sure that there were crawly, slimy creatures digging into my skull. I gritted my teeth and squeezed my fists, to fight off the fear of the terrifying images. I was sure this was the bravest thing I ever did.

The hat was a perfect fit. I shifted it a little to the right, then a little to the back, until it was comfortable. Moments later, my head started to tingle where the edge of the hat touched just above my ears, a soft vibration that gave me a sense of peace, not fear. Papa didn't notice.

"Hey, Keira, I found the answer. Want to know why seagulls can fly?"

"I already know," I said to the surprise of both of us.

"Stop kidding around," Papa said.

"I'm not," I replied. Before he could respond, I continued. "Seagulls' bones, like those of all birds, are hollow and as a result they only weigh a few pounds. Their feathers are light but strong. This allows them to create lift as they flap their wings. Just like when we press our arms and hands against the ground to do a pushup, birds press their wings against the pressure of the air below to push their bodies further into the air."

"That's right," Papa stuttered. "But how did you know that? Did they teach you that in school?"

"We haven't taken that yet. I don't know how I knew it. It just came to me."

Papa removed my hat and studied all sides of it. "The label reads, *Made in Mali*," he said in a whisper.

"It even has the same colors of their flag—green, yellow and red." His tone was like my dad's when he hears a rumor that he can't quite believe. He put it back on my head. "Try this," he said. "What's the capital of the Ivory Coast?"

I placed my chin on my fist like my mom does in deep thought. "Yamoussoukro," I answered. "Holy mackerel! How come I know that?" I yelled.

Papa stood there gazing at me with his mouth open. He stepped back and looked up, searching the skies.

"What are you looking for, Papa? Are you all right?"

"It can't be," Papa whispered.

"What's going on?" I asked. "What can't be?"

"I'm not sure. But I can only think of one reason why you know the answers to these difficult questions. Let me see your hat again."

"Sure," I replied. With unsteady hands I removed the hat and handed it to him.

He hid the hat behind his back and asked, "Who was the third president of the United States? At what temperature does water boil? What is the tallest mountain in the world?"

"I don't have any idea," I responded.

He placed the hat back on my head and repeated the questions.

Without hesitation, I said, "Thomas Jefferson, 212 degrees Fahrenheit, Mount Everest." What! How did I know that? This is too weird."

Papa tried the hat on. He squeezed his eyes tight like I do before opening up a gift, wishing. It didn't work. Papa folded his arms and looked down, his thinking position. I knew not to interrupt him. A few minutes later he raised his head. He looked worried.

"Keira," I am pretty sure that this hat was meant for you to find and for you to wear."

"But why me?" I asked. I don't like to be singled out or the center of attention.

"Keira, I have something important to tell you, something you can never repeat."

"Can I tell my mom and dad?" I asked.

"No, you cannot tell anyone. I know it's not easy to keep a big secret so I will understand if you don't think you can."

I didn't answer right away. Part of me wanted to know because I wanted to tell my friends; that's the best part of a secret. But I liked even more that Papa and I shared secrets together, and that we always kept our promises to each other.

"Papa, you can trust me."

Patting my right hand, he said, "I always have, Gumdrop. I always have." He then gave me a big hug and shared his surprising secret.

"Keira, you know that I worked for the CP Company, living in Africa, Latin America, Asia and the Middle East. What you don't know is that I also worked for the U.S. Government. I was a spy."

I thought Papa was kidding. I expected him to say, "Gotcha." But he continued.

"I am telling you this for two reasons. The first has to do with your hat—which appears to be a magic hat. In West Africa, I befriended a tribal chief in Mali. He had a walking stick that gave him similar powers to those the hat gives you. We teamed up together to prevent an overthrow of the government. He was an old man and has since died."

"Papa, maybe he found a way to send his magic to us. That is why the magic hat washed ashore at this beach and at the exact moment we were here." I suggested.

"Not us. He sent the hat for you to find and you alone, Keira. That's why the magic only works when the hat is on your head which brings me to the second reason I am sharing my secret. I'm bored. I have been ever since I retired five years ago. I miss the action and excitement of new challenges."

"But Papa, why are you now telling me this?"

"I've been thinking about getting back into the spy business," Papa continued. "The magic hat, if used the right way, could help prevent bad things from happening and keep the world safe. Since the magic hat only works for you, I would like you to be my partner. Even without the hat I think you are amazing."

"I don't think I'm amazing, Papa. I tend to avoid new adventures and new challenges. I always imagine that something bad will happen if I try something new." I paused, gaining courage to continue. "I still think that the ball we found might turn into a Cyclops," I admitted.

"Keira, like you, I have a good imagination. I use it to solve problems, not avoid them, something I am sure you can learn to do as well. Together we will be a formidable team. Once you redirect that magnificent imagination of yours toward big ideas and great achievements, we will be the best detective agency ever. Trust me."

That is when The Keira and Papa Detective Agency was formed. That is when I became a spy.

The Call

After taking a phone call, Papa returns to the dining room from his office with a smile and a bounce in his step that wasn't there when he left the table. He's excited—more excited than I've seen him in a long time. It's like the phone call erased his boredom.

He looks me squarely in the eyes. Something's up! He's rubbing his thumb and index finger together. That's his signal to me that a serious problem has occurred somewhere in the world, and our services are needed. That explains Papa's sudden enthusiasm. The Keira and Papa Detective Agency has its first case.

Not wanting to disclose to everyone in the room who called, Papa says, "That was an old friend of mine from Virginia."

"That's nice. Now would you please cut the turkey? We are all starving," Grandma says.

So is my new dog, Waffles, whose tail thumps the floor under the table while he waits for my four-year-old cousin to drop a slice or two. It's Thanksgiving Day. We're at my grandparents' house.

Waffles is short like me. He has furry hair that's the same frosty grey as Papa's. Papa insists he's not related, his ears are not as floppy as Waffles. Papa often cracks me up.

"My old friend is a famous dog trainer in Virginia," Papa says as he begins slicing. Waffles' tail pounds louder. "He owes me a favor. I know it's late notice, but do you think it would be all right if Keira and I fly down to Virginia this weekend? My friend had a last minute dog training cancellation by one of his clients, so there is an opening available. It would be a good opportunity for Waffles to become well behaved if he had a training session with him. We could leave tonight, in fact. There is a 6:00 P.M. flight from White Plains. I checked in case you agreed."

"Can I? Can I?" I shout with false enthusiasm. I know it's important to Papa. As for me, I am not comfortable attempting new things and new adventures. This is very different from the movie theatre imagination that plays films of me as the hero, always saving the day. I guess my imagination is my friend when it comes to daydreaming and my enemy when it comes to actually chasing my daydreams.

"Sure," my mom and dad say at the same time. "But you must be home in time for school on Monday. Remember your class has an outing to the Museum of Natural History," Mom adds.

"Hooray!" I say, still pretending enthusiasm. "But perhaps Grandma needs Papa here," I say, hoping she will say no. "Can he go, Grandma?"

"I suppose so," she says with some hesitation. Papa's smile widens. I begin to sweat.

Grandma gives Papa a suspicious look. "What is he up to?" I hear her mutter to herself.

———

A familiar black limousine arrives on time for our departure. El Gordo is our driver. El Gordo means big in Spanish, which he is. Real big! El Gordo is from Panama. He had worked for Papa there and was instrumental in the capture of the ruthless General Noriega. Now he works for the head of the CIA, General Patti Marco. He has driven us to Washington several times in the past six months for espionage training. Waffles and I like him a lot.

He greets us in his customary jovial manner, "*Buenas tardes, senorita Keira y senior Papa* (Good afternoon, Miss Keira and Mr. Papa)."

I respond, "*Igualmente*, El Gordo (same to you, El Gordo)."

El Gordo looks around with protective eyes as we climb into the back of the limousine. Waffles starts sniffing. He smells something that he can eat. His tail is spinning faster then I have ever seen before. The inside of the limo is more like my living room than a car. It's large enough for Waffles to pick up speed as he circles inside the car in search of the origin of the smell. He knows there is something he wants somewhere, like I do on Christmas morning.

"Sit, Waffles!" I scold without effect. I finally grab him onto my lap and hold him next to Kaya, my American Girl ™ doll. Kaya is more than just a doll. She's more like a robot. Papa had installed gadgets inside her body that I invented with the help of my magic hat. One is a microcomputer and information-seeking device that tells us all kinds of secret information. Perhaps I will get to use it on our first case. The thought of it makes me nervous. I just know something will go wrong.

The Case

The limousine is like a playground on wheels. It has buttons and secret compartments everywhere. As soon as I get in the car I search for the bag of Oreo cookies I know El Gordo has hidden. Waffles gets there first. He's now totally out of control, jumping into the air—all four feet leaving the ground.

"Waffles, I'm sorry, but you know chocolate is not good for dogs," I say.

"Not to worry," El Gordo says. He removes a dog treat hidden just behind the cookies. Waffles is back in the air again. A treat that tastes great and smells like chocolate is his favorite combination.

As I watch Waffles devour his treat, I ask Papa, "What's up? What's really going on? Where are we headed?"

"Do you know what the Crown Jewels are?" he asks.

"No, but wait," I respond as I put on my magic hat. "The Crown Jewels are a collection of swords, rings, crowns and other jewels worn by British kings, queens, princes and princesses during special ceremonies. Each one is decorated with diamonds, rubies and other gems. Some of them are hundreds of years old. They are worth a lot of money."

"Amazing," Papa says. "Well, they were stolen!"

"So Papa, that wasn't your good friend from Virginia on the phone, was it?" I ask.

"No, it was General Marco. She assigned us to a case in England, working with our old friend Commissioner Lamb," he responds. "I called Commissioner Lamb after I hung up with the general to get the details."

The Commissioner is the person in charge of the London police department, the Scotland Yard. He is an old friend of Papa's. Commissioner Lamb visits us in the United States often. He is like family; I call him Uncle Commish. I thought "commissioner" was too long a name for an uncle. I only wish he wasn't so serious. He seems sad.

Waffles jumps from my lap and leaps toward the front seat to be next to El Gordo, expecting another treat. He doesn't see the glass partition. He smacks into it and falls to the floor. He looks around to see if anyone noticed. I pay no attention to him. He sulks. I continue my conversation with Papa.

"How is Uncle Commish?" I ask.

"Not good. The Crown Jewels are a symbol of safety and security to the people of England. Not unlike the Liberty Bell is to us, or for that matter, your cousin's pacifier is to him," Papa says.

I have my magic hat on so I know that the Liberty Bell is a symbol of our country's independence in 1776.

I remove my hat as Papa continues, "The jewels are important to all the people of England. Their Queen expects us to find them and the person who stole them."

The Missing Jewels

"What do we know so far?" I ask. I cross my arms and crunch up my face so I look important, like a spy. "Were all the jewels stolen, Papa?"

"No, what is missing, however, are the most valuable and historical pieces, including the Sovereign's Sceptre with its 530-carat diamond, the Imperial State Crown with its 317-carat diamond, and the 13th century Anointing Spoon, the oldest piece in the collection."

"How much money are they worth?" I ask.

"Putting a value on them is impossible. They're just too special to warrant a price tag. That's what is known as priceless. You know, like you," Papa says as he ruffles my hair.

Waffles grabs my shoe off my foot and starts tearing at it like it's a leather bone. He wants attention and his sulking wasn't getting him any. "Stop it, Waffles! Right this minute!" I scold, and turn back to talk to Papa.

"How big is a 530-carat diamond?" I ask. I am astonished, since my mom's diamond ring is two carats and I think that's big.

"About the size of a baseball," he says.

"Wow," I say. "Do they have any idea who may have done it?"

"They think it was an inside job. The display cabinets are made from the strongest metal and glass in the world and are still intact, nothing was broken. Someone knew the combinations to the locks."

Waffles jumps on my lap with his face six inches from mine—his way of demanding that I play with him. I stare back without a word. He blinks and returns to the floor, his feelings hurt. He can be so dramatic. I give him a loving pat and resume quizzing Papa.

"Is there someone they think did it?" I ask.

"Yes, the Director of the Tower of London, Nathan Shallow."

"Why him?"

Papa explains, "The Director is in charge of security at the Tower of London. The protection of the Crown Jewels is his responsibility, so he has access to them. Apparently he owes a lot of money. His wife, a former beauty queen, demands expensive clothes, a fancy car and a big house. More than he can afford. To pay for it, he borrowed money from a loan shark, a gangster. The money is now due. If he doesn't pay up he will be killed by these bad guys."

"If they know he did it, why don't they arrest him?" I ask.

"Because if they do, they are afraid they will never recover the jewels. Their only hope is that you and I will find them. The Queen of England is counting on us. We can't let her down."

I felt a shutter in me—gangsters, being killed by bad guys? What has Papa got me—us, into? Waffles and me are not cut out for this.

The Plane

We pull up to the jet General Marco made available for us. Captain Virote is there to greet us. He is from Thailand, a country in Asia. Virote worked for Papa in Bangkok, where they uncovered a major drug smuggling operation. He greets us with the traditional *wai* (pronounced why), which is equivalent to a polite handshake. I respond with the same slight bow and my palms pressed together in prayer-like fashion. I say, "*Sa-wat-dee-kah*," which means hello in the Thai language. He smiles at my appreciation for his culture, and the respect I show him.

Waffles races past Virote, up the stairs and onto the plane. He jumps into the front seat next to the co-pilot, Dick Lasus. Waffles' tail is circling like a propeller. When he sees Dick, he leaps over the throttle and onto Dick's lap, licking his face, Waffles entire body wiggling; instant pals. He returns to the pilot's seat and isn't happy when Captain Virote scoots him out and off the plane.

"Sorry, my little friend, dogs are not allowed to fly directly into England. They have to go into quarantine for six months first," Virote explains as though he is talking to a person, like I do with my imaginary friend.

"He's just a puppy. Surely they will allow a puppy," I say. "We can't leave without him, we just can't!"

"It's OK," Papa says after overhearing Virote's conversation with Waffles and my plea not to leave without him. "We have a special exemption from the Queen of England herself for Waffles to enter the country without going into quarantine."

"Hooray!" I shout.

"That is quite unusual, I must admit," Virote says without emotion and goes about his pre-flight check routine.

I love the plane. It flies faster and higher than the regular planes I've been on. It has three compartments. The front is the cockpit, where the pilot and co-pilot fly the plane. In the back are sleeping quarters and bathroom. The main cabin is between the cockpit and the sleeping quarters. It is divided into two sections. One is wood paneled and has large leather seats; it's like a luxurious living room. The other is a science lab. This is where I was trained to use my magic hat to invent formulas and technical devices.

The plane is kept at the White Plains airport, just twenty minutes from Papa's house. We would frequently sneak off for training there. We always had a good excuse for the hours we were gone. The plane is called the *Flying Lab*.

I say goodbye to El Gordo with an *abrazo*, a hug with a couple of pats on the back. He has to kneel down for me to do this. He is not joining us on this trip. Our lives are not at risk. Waffles gives El Gordo a couple of licks. He thinks this will ensure him more tasty chocolate-scented treats when he returns.

We all take our seats and buckle up. I hold Waffles in my lap. I will have to design a special seat belt for him. I won't be able to use my magic hat for this; it's against the rules. I can only use the hat for solving crimes of great importance and not for my own personal needs—like I thought about doing once.

Last year I took an intelligence test for school. When I entered the classroom I wore my magic hat. I knew this was wrong, but I figured, who would know? Plus, I wanted to make my mom and dad proud of me. I stared down at the exam on the desk in front of me. The first question, *"Why can birds fly?"* reminded me of my pledge to Papa, the day we chased the seagulls. I tucked the hat back under my shirt. A promise is a promise!

The Flying Lab taxies to the runway. We start to pick up speed, the land flashes by faster and faster, and the sound of the engines grunt like a weight lifter's all-or-nothing final push. The pressure from the jolt of speed forces my head back into the headrest. Soon we are leveling off and on our way, not to Virginia to train Waffles, but to England... to solve *The Case of the Missing Crown Jewels.*

What have I got myself into?

The Lab

The plane levels off at 45,000 feet. I unbuckle my seatbelt and go right to the lab. I am working on a project of great importance to me. My American Girl Doll, Kaya, has a stain on her right cheek, just under the wax that protects her. I've tried to remove the blemish with the cleaning products sold in the supermarket but they don't work. I must create a formula to remove the stain so she doesn't look different. I'm concerned that it might make her feel self-conscious, like I do sometimes—I have red hair, freckles, wear cool glasses and I'm shorter than my friends.

You may think I'm a little old for dolls. But Kaya isn't like any doll and has been a friend for years. Unlike me, she looks forward to new adventures. Kaya goes everywhere; she is the perfect sidekick. She sees things that Papa and I don't!

Kaya is a member of The Keira and Papa Detective Agency team, so I know Papa won't object if I wear my magic hat to find a way to remove the stain. However, to make sure, I go to the back of the plane to ask him. It sounds like trumpets honking; Papa is snoring. Waffles is afraid of thunder. He hides.

"Papa, can I wear my magic hat to find a way to remove the stain on Kaya?"

Papa grunts, then rolls onto his side.

I shake him lightly and repeat the question.

He snorts a couple of times then mumbles, "Yes, now let me get some sleep. We have a big case to solve."

"Thank you." I say. "Good night, Papa." I give him a light kiss on the cheek. He smiles. He is so excited to be back in the spy business. I'm glad he isn't bored anymore.

I start experimenting with different formulas. I mix several chemicals and heat them in a beaker, something I am only allowed to do when I have my magic hat on. After several attempts, I think I have what I need and dab a little of the formula on Kaya's cheek. "This won't hurt," I whisper like Dr. Collins does before the needle, only I am telling the truth.

Within seconds the stain is gone. "I did it!" I shout to myself. "Oops. Sorry, magic hat, we did it!"

I am not ready to sleep. I decide to watch a movie, *Tangled*, my favorite. First I go to the refrigerator for a glass of milk and to the secret compartment where Dick, the co-pilot hid the oatmeal cookies. Waffles had found them within minutes of re-boarding the plane. Papa had told me earlier that it would be OK if I had a snack after we were airborne. Waffles snuggles up on my lap between the bag of oatmeal cookies and Kaya.

I must have been more tired than I thought. I am deep into a dream when Dick wakes me up. "We are preparing to land," he says. Too bad, in my dream I was about to score the winning goal for our soccer team.

As I become fully alert, I see that the glass of milk is still full but the entire bag of cookies is gone. Funny, I don't remember eating any of them. Uh, oh. "Waffles, where are you?"

He sticks his crumb-filled face out from behind a chair. "What did you do, Waffles? What did you do?" I say, pretending to sound serious.

He must not be feeling well as he meanders over to me. I have to pick him up. He's too full to jump, but not too full to cover my face with oatmeal kisses. All is forgiven.

During our landing approach, I hold Waffles and Kaya as tight as I can. I think they are nervous, like I am. To comfort them, and me, I say with more confidence than I feel, "Now don't you worry. Captain Virote is the best pilot in the whole world." Then, with less confidence, I talk about *The Case of the Missing Crown Jewels.* "Kaya, I expect you to help me solve this case. Papa is sure we can do it." I wish I were.

5

The Commish

We land at the Royal Air Force base. It's 7:00 A.M. Sir Hazledine, the Private Secretary to the Queen, is there to greet us. He wears a dark suit. It has a ribbon with a medal pinned to it. Although his hair is receding, his mustache is quite healthy—he has a giant mustache. When he sees me, it springs out like wings.

Sir Hazledine

"You are only a child," he says, astonished.

"And I am pleased to meet you too, Sir Hazledine," I giggle.

After exchanging pleasantries, Papa explains the reason for my presence. Sir Hazledine is not convinced; he rolls his eyes.

"Her Majesty the Queen requests that we meet her at Buckingham Palace. She insists that she be involved," the Secretary announces. "Does the Queen know that Keira is a mere child?" he adds.

"Yes," Papa says and turns to me.

"Keira, if we are going to meet the Queen, you will need to wear the pink dress Grandma gave you for your birthday."

"But Papa, I never wear a dress, so I didn't pack it," I respond, happy I won't have to wear it. I prefer multi-layers and lots of colors. Grandma calls it my peacock look.

"Good news," Papa says with a knowing smirk. "I packed it for you." Papa's tricky.

During the forty-five minute ride, Sir Hazledine explains, in a very formal voice, the importance of confidentiality and Royal protocol.

"Keira, have you ever met a Queen before?" he asks in a doubtful tone. Apparently Sir Hazledine doesn't have a high opinion of children. I can tell he doesn't like me.

"Not really," I answer softly.

Secretary Hazledine then explains to Papa and me how to greet the Queen. This is different from the American handshake, El Gordo's *abrazo* and Virote's *wai*. I am to curtsy. I do this by extending the sides of my skirt out while bending my right knee and stretching my left leg back and behind my right leg. He also advises that when one leaves the Queen's presence, one walks backwards out of the room so as to never turn one's back on her. Sir Hazledine instructs that protocol requires we address the Queen as Your Majesty when we first meet. Subsequently we may also call her Ma'am.

The car is large, so for the remainder of the ride I practice my curtsy, as does Kaya. Waffles thinks this is a game. He tries to bow but tumbles over each time. I am a little worried what Waffles may do when he meets the Queen.

Commissioner Lamb is waiting for us outside the palace front door when the Rolls Royce enters the courtyard. I leap out of the car and run into Uncle Commish's open arms. He is pleased to see that Kaya also made the trip; she was his gift to me when I was a little girl. He knows about the mini-computer and special devices we installed in her.

Papa and the Commissioner embrace, then kiss each other on each cheek. This is a French custom from their days together in the Ivory Coast. The Commissioner once rescued Papa when a spy operation in West Africa went wrong. Papa lost part of his left ear that time.

Waffles shoots out from the back seat, heading directly for one of the ponds on the property. "Stop, Waffles! Stop, please stop!" I shout in a voice meant to let him know I am serious, like my dad does with me. "Papa, Waffles has my hat in his mouth!"

Sir Hazledine chases after him but he is not fast enough. Waffles leaps through the air and into the water. He is not graceful like a swan. He is more like the boys in my class showing off with cannonballs off the diving board.

Uncle Commish is bent over in laughter. "What a funny dog. I wish I had a photo of Secretary Hazledine chasing after him. Bravo, Waffles." I love it when Uncle Commish laughs. I wish he did it more often.

Sir Hazledine returns Waffles to me, clearly annoyed. "You should learn to control your dog," he says. "In England, we expect our dogs, and children ... to behave." I think he's stuffy.

"Bad Waffles! Bad Waffles!" I repeat as I dry him off. My hat is drenched and torn. I'm afraid to test my magic hat. I'm sure it is ruined. In his playfulness he ripped the hat almost in two. I'm worried that this may have shorted out all its magical qualities.

"Keira," Papa says as he pulls me aside, away from the others, put your hat on." He looks worried too.

I do as he says. I hope he thinks that the water now running down my cheeks is from the pond.

"What is the symbol for gold?" Papa asks.

I try to think with all my might, but I come up blank. "I don't know," I respond.

"Who invented the violin?" he continues.

"I don't know," I repeat, my voice cracking.

"How big is the galaxy?" Papa asks, with less hope in his voice.

Papa now sees that it is not water from my hat that is gushing down my face.

"Keira, don't cry. Don't worry, everything will be all right," Papa says with confidence.

"But if I don't have the magic hat, we won't be able to solve the case and you won't want me to be your partner," I sniffle.

The Queen

"Keira, I don't care if the magic is gone, you will always be my partner. You are special with or without the hat," he says.

The Commissioner, who has been silent, says, "Sorry, but the Queen is waiting to meet you and her schedule is quite tight."

"Give us a couple of minutes," Papa says to him. "We'll meet you at the entrance."

"Keira," Papa says to me, "I know you are disappointed that you have lost your special magic, but you cannot let that keep you down and sad. You need to think of this as a new opportunity. This will be a good challenge for you to put that amazing imagination of yours to good use. So get over your disappointment, and look forward to the challenge ahead."

I look at Waffles whose tail is in full spin, as though all is great. He's happy. Being with Papa and me is enough for him. Perhaps Waffles is smarter than I thought.

If Papa thinks I can still be a good spy, even without my hat, that's enough for me. I make a pledge to myself to stop always thinking the worst.

"OK, Papa. I will do my best." I wipe away my disappointment, stand straight and tell myself, "I can do this. I'm twelve and I'm tough." Then I sneak in, "I hope."

We catch up with the Commissioner and go directly to the receiving area.

We enter what is called the White Drawing Room. It is the most beautiful room I have ever seen. The ceiling is as high as my school gym. The walls are painted gold with white trim. Hand carved molding decorate the walls. There is a picture of a Queen from long ago. The Queen's desk is also in the room. It's magnificent. Her Majesty rises as we enter. I don't see her at first, as I am staring at the walls and ceiling. I am thinking about how great it would be to be queen and to live in such a beautiful home.

Sir Hazledine clears his throat to get my attention.

"Oh, hi!" I say to Her Majesty, forgetting what Sir Hazledine had instructed. "Oh, I'm sorry, Your Majesty. This room is so beautiful!"

The Queen smiles and says, "Your skirt is lovely," in response to my curtsy.

Although she is formal, she's nice. I think it must be hard to walk around with all the heavy-looking clothes she's wearing. She looks down at my arms and asks, "What a sweet puppy, what's his name?"

"Waffles," I reply, as he jumps from my arms and races across the room to investigate a dog lying in the sun next to a giant window that rises from the floor to the ceiling. Sir Hazledine coughs lightly, to remind me of how dogs and children should behave.

"Is that your dog, Ma'am?" I ask.

"Actually, it's my husband's dog. His name is Horace." I think that's a silly name for a dog, but I keep my opinion to myself. I don't want to hurt her feelings.

"What kind of dog is it?" I ask.

Her Majesty says, "It's a Lab. As for me, I prefer a Welsh corgi. I have owned thirty since I was a child. I just love dogs." I really like the Queen.

Something bothers Waffles, and he starts barking furiously at Horace. I am so embarrassed. I run over and pick Waffles up to calm him down. He's suddenly quiet. I think he is sulking, like my sister does sometimes if she doesn't get her way. Waffles never acted this way before. I wish I knew what caused him to be angry at the royal Lab. I also wish Sir Hazledine wasn't staring at me so sternly.

The Governor

The Queen introduces us to the Governor of the Tower of London, the man responsible for the safety of the jewels. He steps forward, relying on his cane to keep his balance.

"Ouch!" I shout, his grip way too tight when we shake hands.

Waffles growls.

"So sorry, little girl!" he exclaims. He speaks with a funny accent, different from the Queen's and the Commissioner's accent.

"What country are you from?" I ask. "You don't sound like the other English people I have met." Papa looks at me, surprised by my forwardness, and I am too.

The Queen laughs. This makes me feel dumb. Waffles senses this and licks my face. I guess the Queen realizes that she hurt my feelings. She says, "Oh, Keira, I am not laughing at you because you said something silly, quite the opposite. In fact, I am laughing because we always tease the Governor about his funny accent. It was clever of you to notice it so quickly."

The Queen goes on to explain that when the Governor was a child, he lived for many years outside of England. His father had been a highly decorated member of the diplomatic corps, having held Ambassadorships on three continents. Her Majesty says, "I remember when I appointed the Governor's father to his first Ambassadorship. The Governor was about your age, Keira. He even had red hair like you do. As did his... oh, never mind." She stops suddenly. "It's the recovery of the Crown Jewels that we need to talk about," she continues.

I stand straighter, shoulders back, head held high, and my arms folded on my chest—my favorite spy position. "Your Majesty, were the Crown Jewels always kept in the same vault?" I begin.

"Good question," she replies. "Up until 1671, they were secured in the Martin Tower."

Waffles wiggles in my arms. He has his eyes focused on Sir Hazledine for some reason. Sir Hazledine shakes his head as if to say no, and then looks the other way.

"Perhaps I could hold Waffles," Uncle Commish suggests, as he sees me struggle to keep Waffles still. He takes him from my arms.

"The Martin Tower!" I say. "That's your name, Papa." Kiddingly I say, "Did you use to own the Tower of London?" Uncle Commish smiles.

"No, Keira. I am not quite that old!" Papa says with a pretend serious voice.

"Why did they move the jewels from the Martin Tower, Your Majesty?" I continue.

"There was an attempted theft by Colonel Thomas Blood, way back in 1671. He was caught, and to the surprise of all, King Charles pardoned the culprit. That is when they built the Jewel House. It was located inside the walls of the Tower of London to ensure that the jewels would always be safe," the Queen explains. She nods her head slightly toward Commissioner Lamb for him to continue.

"Right," Uncle Commish says. "Since then, MI6, England's secret service police had installed the most advanced security technology in existence. At the request of Scotland Yard, alarms, cameras and sensing devices are hidden everywhere. We were assured that nothing could ever leave the vault." His shoulders slump.

"Finding the Crown Jewels is only half the problem," the Queen continues. "The Crown Jewels are more than a collection of jewels worn by British kings, queens, princes and princesses. Together they tell the story of England's proud history; they are the symbol that holds the country together in good times and bad. We not only have to recover them quickly, we cannot let word get out that they are missing."

"Keira," the Queen says, "I am counting on you and your grandfather to solve the greatest jewel theft in history."

The Commissioner says, "Ma'am, I am quite confident that Keira and her grandfather will solve the case in a week."

"Uncle Commish!" I say. The Queen smiles when she hears my nickname for the solemn Commissioner Lamb. "We have to solve the case by late Sunday. I have school on Monday."

Then reality sets in; my magic hat doesn't work.

The Tower

The Queen requests that Secretary Hazledine drive us to the Tower of London. We are to follow behind the Governor and Commissioner, each of whom has his own vehicle. There are also police cars in front of and behind us. It's like a parade. The Queen waves goodbye to us from behind the large window, tilting her hand from left to right. Waffles looks back and sees the Lab sitting next to her and growls.

"Waffles stop that!" I scold. "Horace is a perfectly nice dog. What's wrong with you, anyway?" Embarrassed, I turn toward Sir Hazledine and suggest that the next time he should give protocol lessons to Waffles.

"I don't think there are enough lessons in the world to help your dog," he says.

"Sir Hazledine, you know you hurt my feelings when you say bad things about Waffles. It's not very nice."

He grumbles.

A fog has rolled in; it's hard to see out the windows. Traffic moves slowly. Waffles naps on my lap, cuddled up next to my doll, Kaya. "Is it always so grey and rainy?" I ask the Secretary.

"The sun is bad for the skin," he replies.

"What? That's a funny answer," I whisper to Kaya. "I think Sir Hazledine must like riddles."

"Oh-oh," I say. "It's starting to rain hard."

"Don't worry," Sir Hazledine says. "I keep a brolly in my boot."

I look at Papa for help. I don't have a clue as to what Sir Hazledine means. Papa whispers, "A brolly is an umbrella."

"What?" I shout, loud enough for everyone to hear. "Sir Hazledine keeps an umbrella in his boot? That makes no sense."

"Oh my," the Secretary says.

"Keira," Papa says, "although both our countries speak English, there are some words and expressions that have different meanings. A boot in this case means the trunk of a car, not what we wear on our feet."

"Oh!" I say, and then change the subject. "Are we almost there?"

"Keira," the Secretary says, "do you know how old the Tower of London is?"

Papa interrupts and tells me to put on my hat. "It's cold," he says with a wink.

Papa must have forgotten that Waffles ruined the hat, and that its magic is finished.

"It's ripped Papa. It doesn't work," I whisper.

Papa insists that I put it on. He says, "While you and the Queen were having your private chat, I patched the hat back together with duct tape. Please put it on, your mother will be upset with me if you return with a cold."

My dad uses duct tape to fix everything, so it figures Papa would do the same. I doubt that it can restore the magic, but I do as he asks. I take the hat in both hands and pull it down on my head from back to front. It feels a little tighter.

"I'm sorry, Sir Hazledine, would you please repeat your question?" I ask.

"Of course," he says, perhaps taking note of my politeness. "How old is the Tower of London?"

I look down at my feet. Then, slowly, I raise my head and look at Papa. He tilts his head slightly to the right, his way of encouraging me to continue.

"The Tower of London is over one thousand years old. William the Conqueror built it after capturing England in 1066. The United States didn't even exist then."

"Correct," Secretary Hazledine says with a note of surprise.

If only I could tell Dad that duct tape really can fix anything.

I see the Tower of London as we drive over Tower Bridge. It is surrounded by high walls and looks out over the River Thames. The buildings are old and the walls are several feet thick. It looks more like a village, with all the homes inside the walls. That is where the staff lives.

"Hooray, look at the Beefeaters standing guard!" I shout with excitement as I see the tower ahead. "I love their red and black uniforms. I wish our policemen had uniforms like that."

Beefeaters

"I am surprised that you know this. I am pleased that you like them," Sir Hazledine replies.

As we drive through the gates, I see Beefeaters everywhere. I think it would be difficult to steal something from the Tower of London. There are two guards on either side of the entrance. They never smile or move. I'm told that part of the fun of visiting the Tower of London is trying to make them smile. No one has done it yet.

The Governor and Commissioner are waiting as we pull up to the building that houses the Crown Jewels. Something's wrong. Uncle Commish looks angry.

The Fakes

The Governor leads us through the entrance. The cobblestone flooring is uneven, making it difficult for the Governor to maintain his balance. It is slow going, but with Waffles and Kaya in my arms, the relaxed pace is fine with me. At last the Governor leads us through the front entrance. Papa's whole body stiffens at what he sees.

Just inside the entrance door there is a yellow tent sign that reads:

CAUTION!
WET FLOORS

Apparently every Thursday night the floors of the Tower are waxed, including the vault where the Crown Jewels are displayed.

The sign means nothing to Waffles. He charges into the room, skidding and spinning on the freshly waxed floors, his legs finally spreading in all directions until he flops face first onto the floor.

He looks like a tiny bear rug. Although this is funny, his timing is bad.

Mischievous Waffles

"All the prints from the crime scene are ruined. They are covered with wax! It will be impossible to solve the crime! How could this have happened?" Papa grumbles. He is furious.

Commissioner Lamb explains. "Do you remember the Queen's parting words to us, "We not only have to recover them quickly, we cannot let word out that they are missing?"

"Yes, of course," Papa answers. "Go on."

"When we first learned that the jewels were missing, we understood immediately that the first challenge was to prevent the public from knowing," the Commissioner explains.

"I don't understand. What does that have to do with waxing the floors?" Papa says.

The Commissioner continues, "When we enter the vault, you will see the Crown Jewels on display. They are not real."

My jaw drops.

"They are fakes, counterfeit, duplicates as old as the originals," he says. "It is a custom that was started over one thousand years ago by King William I. The duplicates have been and still are displayed at state dinners, where foreigners are seldom trusted. Only a few important people know of their existence, including the Governor and me."

"Oh, I get it," I say. "As far as anyone knows, the Crown Jewels were never stolen. But how did you do that?"

"Shortly after the Governor and I arrived at the scene yesterday," Commissioner Lamb says, "we summoned the entire staff to assemble outside the entrance of the building. We explained to them that we had been alerted to a potential attempt to steal the Crown Jewels. I told them that, as a precaution, I had a team of secret agents relocate our country's greatest treasure to the hidden royal vaults. While I explained this, I had MI6 (a branch of the secret service) retrieve the duplicates and place them in the display cabinets. That is what the staff saw when they resumed their posts. As far as they know, the Jewels are not missing."

"I see," Papa says softly. "That explains why standard protocol for protecting evidence—crime tape, extra security, all entry forbidden—couldn't be followed. You had to maintain a sense that all was normal."

"That is correct," the Governor says with a note of arrogance.

"But still, without prints, it will be impossible to solve this case," Papa says in a discouraged voice.

I take hold of his hand. "Please don't worry. I will find a solution." Recalling Papa's advice to me earlier that morning, I say, "It's just the challenge I'm looking for!"

Papa squeezes my hand gently. "I know you will," he says to me, his voice calmer. "And thank you for reminding me. We will approach this as an opportunity." He gives me the I think you are amazing look.

"Governor," I say, "who is responsible for the cleaning of this building?"

"That would be Director Shallow," he replies. "But we can't hold him responsible for this. As far as he and his staff know, the fake jewels that now sit in the vault are real."

"Unless Director Shallow was the one who stole them," I respond.

The Director

We already knew from Papa's Thanksgiving Day conversation with Commissioner Lamb that Director Shallow was the Commissioner's primary suspect. After observing the Director's strange behavior on the day of the theft, the Commissioner had ordered a full investigation. He reminds us of his findings as we proceed to the Director's office. The Director's wife, a former beauty queen, spends more money than he makes, and the Director is in serious financial trouble. He needs to obtain a lot of money and quickly. His life depends on it. We now learn that Director Shallow owes a gangster the equivalent of one million dollars, and the total is due next Friday.

The Director jumps to attention as we enter his office. "Nice to have you back," he says to the Commissioner. "You probably want to check to make sure that the Crown Jewels are safe. I don't blame you. That was quite a scare we had yesterday."

"No," the Commissioner declares, continuing his charade. "I am sure they are safe and sound. However, the Queen wants to make sure that they continue to be safe."

"Quite understandable," he replies. He glances up at Papa and down at me. He's nervous. He offers us a chocolate from the large box on his desk.

I look up at Papa hopefully. Waffles' tail is whipping around. Waffles has forgotten that chocolate is dangerous for dogs to eat.

"No, thank you," Papa and Commissioner Lamb say in unison.

The Director shrugs his shoulders and tosses a couple of pieces into his elastic-like mouth. Maybe he eats when he is nervous. He's huge. He must weigh at least three hundred pounds.

"I have with me an investigator who will conduct the audit of the security systems," the Commissioner explains. "Director Shallow, this is Mr. Jones." The Commissioner doesn't use Papa's real name, nor does he provide the name of the agency, nor does he mention me. Our secret is safe.

I notice the Director's shortness of breath and the fact that his clothes are wet from sweat. He takes another chocolate.

"Sorry, I didn't expect you," the Director says.

"Please excuse me while I freshen up. I feel a little under the weather today."

After he leaves the room, I ask Uncle Commish, "Is that a picture of a previous Queen of England on the Director's desk?"

"No," he replies. "That is a picture of his wife. As I mentioned, she is a former beauty queen."

"How come there are no pictures of him or his children?" I continue. I am now a sleuth asking questions—I don't need my hat for this, I'm a natural.

"He doesn't have any children," the Commissioner says. "His whole life is built around his wife. He wears his marriage to a beauty queen like an accessory."

"What?" I say. "That makes no sense. How can a person be an accessory? He can't wear her around his neck."

"You are right, he can't. In this case it is more like someone who thinks he or she is more important because they drive a big expensive car. They think that if they are seen driving the car, people will assume they are special."

"Oh, I get it. It's like some of the kids in my class who hang around with the most popular kid because they think that will make them cool."

"Exactly," Uncle Commish responds.

I think about the facts relating to the Director and his strange behavior for a few minutes. Something tells me that we might be on the wrong track.

"Papa, I don't think the Director could have taken the jewels."

"Why is that?" Papa asks.

"Well," I answer, "for two reasons. First, he is too nervous. To commit a crime like this would require a soldier's courage."

"OK, but what's the second reason?" Papa inquires.

"You'd have to have a lot of self-confidence to steal the Crown Jewels. At school, kids who think they are cool because they hang around with the most popular person usually aren't confident in themselves."

Uncle Commish ruffles my hair and says, "You are a bright one."

I blush and lower my head. Compliments make me feel uncomfortable. Besides, I don't think I am that bright.

The Director returns, looking a little better. He takes another chocolate. I sit quietly in the corner of his office while the adults talk. I think about the liquid formula I developed that penetrated the wax on Kaya's face to remove the stain underneath. I slip on my hat, and *Presto!*

I am sure that, with a slight modification, my formula can be used to penetrate the newly waxed floor of the Tower. If I were to add dye, I reason, it might be able to reveal a footprint—human or otherwise. I email our pilot, Captain Virote, requesting that he purchase for me three extra ingredients I will need to produce the revised formula that might solve the case.

"Keira," Papa announces, "the Director is going to take us on a tour of the Tower."

"Coming, Papa." I can't wait to tell him my idea. Maybe Papa is right. Maybe I can do this.

"Leave Waffles with me," Uncle Commish suggests. "We don't need to disturb the crime scene any more than we have to."

The Vault

There is no need for the Governor and the Commissioner to accompany us on our tour, so we agree to meet back at the Governor's office at 4:00 P.M. As the Director leads us from room to room, he introduces us to each Beefeater on duty, explaining the reason for our presence. No one is suspicious. Everyone understands the need for an audit of the security systems.

We then enter the vault that displays the Crown Jewels. I put my magic hat back on. The door is two feet thick. The floor is slate, not wood or cobblestone as it is in the rest of the building. There are no jewels to be seen as we first enter, only photos of queens, kings, crowns, and some beautiful plates. Then we turn right into the next area and presto, there are all the items on display. They don't look fake.

A moving walkway takes us past five cabinets, one of which contains the counterfeit Sovereign's

Sceptre. It looks like a wand from Cinderella. We then reach the last display cabinet, where the original Imperial State Crown had been exhibited. The imitation sitting in its place draws no suspicion. Everything looks perfect. The counterfeit jewels on display appear genuine to all concerned.

Papa and I repeat our examination of the room several times, unsuccessful in our effort to find clues. At one point, I am no longer a spy and begin to imagine myself as the Queen and Kaya as a princess. I picture us at an orphanage. The children all look so sad that I decide to adopt them all. "Hooray!" I hear them shouting. But now I am back in reality. It is Papa who is saying, "Hurry!" not the orphans shouting "Hooray." We head to the Governor's office empty-handed.

The Governor's office is elegant. There are large expensive paintings of landscapes and family portraits hanging on the walls throughout the room. The beautiful hand-woven silk rugs scattered on the shiny wood floor attract Waffles' attention.

"Don't even think about it," I say, knowing that he needs a walk in the garden.

Uncle Commish, who is still holding Waffles, comes to his defense. "You wouldn't do that now, would you, boy?" He laughs.

The Governor's ornate desk is enormous. The high-back leather chair behind it reminds me of the Wicked Queen's throne in Snow White. The desk is clear of papers. The diplomas on the wall read Eton and Cambridge, which my hat tells me are the best of the best schools in England.

"Papa," I whisper, "the Governor is an extraordinary person, isn't he?"

Papa gives me that *don't rush to reach an opinion* look.

"Oh, right," I remember. "You can hide a lot of rubbish behind a rosebush."

"Amazing," he mutters.

The Governor offers tea as he invites us to take a seat. The Commissioner paces the floor, anxious to learn if we had made any progress. We explain that we were unsuccessful in the investigation of the crime scene. For two hours we exchange theories based on the sparse information we have each collected. Nothing resonates. Without footprints, the outlook is bleak. We agree to regroup tomorrow at 10:00 A.M. in the Governor's office. Papa and I need time to assess the limited information we have collected and to tap into Papa's network of spies and flies. Spies work for the government. They are good guys. Flies are bad guys trying to be good. They share secret information about criminals and criminal plots to avoid going to jail.

We are about to leave when I take notice of the photo of the Governor with his wife and two children. His wife is beautiful.

"What is that your wife is wearing?" I ask the Governor. "She is beautiful, as is your whole family."

"Thank you, my dear," he says. "The picture you reference was taken outside our church. My wife is the priest of our Church of England parish. In America, you'd say Episcopal. I am quite proud of her." He touches the silver picture frame softly, his hand shaking slightly. His eyes water suggesting that he might be upset. I wonder why the family photo shakes him.

Suddenly I feel a little better about this arrogant man. Anyone who loves his family so much and whose wife is a priest must have something nice about him.

Waffles growls.

The Surprise

Sir Hazledine is parked at the entrance, waiting to drive us back to our plane. We always stay in the plane because of the science laboratory and the advanced security equipment that protects our communications.

I feel all fidgety inside. I can't wait to get to the plane so I can tell Papa about my formula idea. I can't tell him in the car. Not even Sir Hazledine knows about my magic hat.

"Keira," Papa says, "you're excited about something. What is it?"

"It's a surprise. Shush!" I say, holding my index finger to my lips.

Papa looks at me, squeezes his lips together and crunches his shoulders up—his way of saying, "What's up?" without talking.

"Sir Hazledine, do you have children?" I ask.

"No. I do not!" he responds.

"Don't you like children?" I ask.

"I find them quite annoying. That's one of the aspects I like about serving the Royal family. It keeps me away from the little rascals most of the time," he says as he glances back at me just as we arrive at our plane.

Sir Hazledine holds open the car door for us. Waffles darts out, barking and growling at the plane. I have never seen him so angry. His fury continues to build until finally I get it.

"Papa, do you remember how rude Waffles was to Horace, the royal dog?" I ask.

He nods yes.

"Well, it wasn't until Her Majesty said that he was a Lab that Waffles started to growl," I say.

"You mean that Waffles doesn't like Labs?" Papa asks.

"No, he doesn't like that we named the plane *The Flying Lab*, the same breed as Horace," I say with my magic hat still tucked inside my shirt.

Papa and I laugh. Sir Hazledine is not amused, and bids us a good evening.

I shout back to him, "See ya tomorrow."

He shakes his head and mumbles, "Kids!"

"I don't think the Secretary likes me," I say to Papa, sounding disappointed.

Papa says, "He's just one of those people that doesn't appreciate children. He has nothing against you personally," Papa explains. "Now, what's this big secret of yours that you are so excited about?"

"Papa, my surprise is that I think I have a way of finding the prints under the waxed floors at the Tower of London," I announce.

"Go on," he says.

"Well, Papa, when you were asleep last night, I developed a formula that could remove the stain under Kaya's waxed cheek."

"You did? I didn't hear you," Papa answers.

"Papa, you snore too loudly to hear anything." I chuckle.

"When we were in the Director's office," I continue, "I thought of a way to modify the formula so it would help us solve the case."

"So that is what you were so focused on. I had to call you twice to join us on the tour, in fact," Papa says. "Please continue."

"There were a few new ingredients I needed. I emailed Virote to purchase them for me."

"And I did," Virote says proudly. He hands me a bag marked with skull and crossbones—poison.

"Outstanding," Papa says. "Now at least we have a couple of options to pursue."

After dinner, I put on my magic hat and start working on the formula. Papa is busy making phone calls and surfing the Internet, searching for clues and information.

I like to work with a pencil and paper first. I seem to be more creative and effective when I think through the details without staring at a computer screen. It's past midnight when I am ready to start mixing ingredients. Papa is snoring in the back. Before he went to bed, he told me his efforts to find clues were unsuccessful. He hopes there will be a few callbacks in the morning.

My hand is unsteady holding the test tube as I pour a measured amount into the beaker. I spill a few drops. "Be careful," I say to myself. I can't afford to waste any of the chemicals. I pour the new formula on the counter tile. It doesn't work. "Oh no!"

I only have enough for two more attempts. I worry that the duct tape may not be strong enough to hold in the magic. I pull down the hat a little further on my head, making it tighter, closer to my brain. I make a minor adjustment to the formula and pour the different ingredients into the beaker. A white cloud appears. I am hopeful. Carefully I pour some on the tile again. Failure!

The hat has lost its magic.

The Formula

I only have enough chemicals for one more formula, but my hat isn't functioning as it should. I decide to sleep on it. That's what Papa does when I ask him if I can bring friends up for the weekend. He almost always says yes the next morning, so it must work.

I wake up to Waffles licking my face. It's the middle of the night. He needs to go outside.

"OK, OK, give me a minute," I say. I sound like my mom.

I open the cabin door. It's cool and damp. Without thinking, I put my magic hat on to stay warm. It's dark, scary dark. No stars, no moon. We walk over to the side of the terminal near the garden. I shine the flashlight on a small patch of lawn so Waffles can see. I freeze.

The light is now fixed on the brownish-green moss at the base of a tree.

"That's it!" I shout. I know what's been missing from my formula. The magic hat is working again.

I shave off a small piece of the fungi and return to the lab. I mix the chemicals and heat them in the beaker over the Bunsen burner. I hold my breath.

"This has to work. This has to work," I mutter.

With my fingers crossed I pour the liquid on the slate. I'm nervous, and my confidence has vanished, kind of like I feel when my parents watch me at a guitar recital. I'm afraid to look down. I close my eyes and count to ten. Slowly I open them.

"Oh no!" I cry. My shoulders drop along with my hope of solving the case. The liquid formula remains a puddle on top of the wax that I had applied to the tile. I cover my eyes with both hands and count to ten again, hoping for a miracle.

"Please work," I whisper as I begin to remove one finger at a time. "We have to find the jewels. I cannot disappoint Papa."

The puddle remains. The formula doesn't work. I sink to the floor, the disappointment dragging me down. Then frustration takes hold. At times like this it is hard for me to control my emotions. Papa taught me a technique to help me deal with this. I lie on the floor, resting my head on my arms. I focus on controlling my breathing. At first it's almost impossible but soon my inhales and exhales are steady. Minutes later I am asleep.

The sound of Waffles barking and scratching on the cabin door wakes me up. In my excitement to make the formula with the fungi, I had rushed back to the lab and had forgotten all about Waffles. I had left him outside all this time.

"I'm sorry, Waffles," I say as I open the door. He's not mad. He is only happy to see me.

When he sees how sad I am, his tail stops circling and his eyes droop.

"Oh, Waffles, I've lost my magic. The formula didn't work. Look how it sits on the surface like spilled water on the kitchen floor." I pick him up to show him. I force myself to raise my head from looking down at the floor. I am so disappointed. At first, I don't even notice. I guess I've already determined in my own mind that it wasn't going to work. Then reality sets in. I can't believe my eyes.

"Wait a minute. It's gone. It worked," I say snuggling my nose into Waffles' fur. His tail is in full circle.

I'm so happy. I realize that the formula needed more time to dissolve through the wax. When it did, it outlined in blue the footprint and handprint I had made on the tile. I never would have discovered the fungi if it wasn't for Waffles.

"You deserve a biscuit," I say to him. "If it wasn't for you, I never would have discovered the missing ingredient to my formula. You're the best."

I tiptoe back to my bed, holding Waffles and whispering to Kaya what happened. Papa is still snoring. Waffles looks up at me with worried eyes, as if to say, "how can we sleep with all that racket?" I get the message. We go to the main cabin; the chairs recline flat. I cover us up with a multicolored quilt my great-grandmother had made.

"Good night, Waffles. Good night, Kaya."

All is well—for the moment.

The Prints

Sir Hazledine is waiting with the car as we descend from the plane the next morning. He gives a disapproving look at what I am wearing—a short skirt, with bright red leggings, several layers all with different colors and patterns. and my magic hat with gray duct tape holding it together.

"What's wrong?" I ask, responding to his stare.

"Never mind," he says as he starts the engine. We are off to the Tower of London.

"Keira, is this your first trip to England?" Sir Hazledine asks.

I brighten up, happy that he even acknowledged me. "Yes, but I have read about it. My great-great-grandmother was from Kent."

"Really?" he says, sounding somewhat shocked. "Do you know who else was from Kent?" he continues.

"Lots of people, including Sir Winston Churchill. He was such a great man—a soldier, a journalist, an author, a painter and Prime Minister. He did so much for the world," I say.

We continue to discuss England until we finally arrive at the Tower of London. Sir Hazledine is about to pull away when he stops, rolls down his window and calls me over.

"Keira, I must say I quite enjoyed our little chat," he says with a pleasant smile. "Make a good show of it today. Cheerio!"

"And, cheerio to you too, Sir Hazledine!" It was a good thing that I had my magic hat on. Otherwise I might have thought that he wanted cereal. But in England, "cheerio" means goodbye.

The Governor is on the phone when we arrive at his office. The room is musty; it smells like cigarettes. I guess the no-smoking rule doesn't apply to him. He waves for us to take a seat. I prefer to stand. The chairs are so big I may not be able to find my way out once I am seated.

He completes his call as the Commissioner arrives. They shake hands briefly. The Commissioner smiles when he sees me. He extends a slight bow toward me, like Papa did when he met the Queen. I curtsy in response. I like English tradition. Waffles couldn't care less. He jumps from my arms and runs to Uncle Commish, who catches him in mid-air.

"How's my little friend this morning?" he asks.

Waffles responds with wiggles and licks. Uncle Commish doesn't seem to mind.

"Keira," Papa says, "please describe your invention to the Commissioner and the Governor."

I do as he asks. When I finish, Uncle Commish applauds with great enthusiasm.

The Governor, however, looks irritated." Ridiculous!" he exclaims. "This is a tourist attraction, and there will be hundreds of footprints to sort out. We are wasting our time!"

I can tell by Papa's nodding head that he shares the Governor's concern. I also know by the shade of red his ears have turned that he is not happy with the Governor's rudeness.

"You might be right, but it is worth a try," Papa says to the Governor. "And for the record, nothing my granddaughter suggests is ever ridiculous."

"OK, OK," the Governor replies. "Let's get on with it."

The Governor leads us back to the giant vault from where the jewels had been stolen. His limp is worse than before; he's putting more of his weight on the cane. He dismisses the Beefeater, explaining that we are conducting a product test that is still considered a state secret. The Beefeater's salute is crisp. His shoulders are back, his head held high and his chest out as he marches from the room, proud to be involved, even if only in his dismissal. The Governor taps in a lengthy code to unlock the vault. It doesn't open. The Governor repeats the code, this time taking more care. It opens and a rush of fresh air replaces the dusty smell of the damp room.

"Will you hold Waffles, Uncle Commish, so I have both hands free to work with?" I ask.

"Nothing would make me happier," he says. I can tell he means it.

I remove the bottle from my pocket with care, like I do with loose change. I unscrew the top. The fragrance that escapes smells like honeysuckle. I pour one tablespoon into the bucket of tepid water I had requested. It bubbles as expected. I stir gently. When it stops bubbling, I know it's ready. With a large sponge I cover a ten square foot area. I wait for the miracle. I'm nervous. I feel less confident than before. Within moments the floor lights up with several blue footprints disclosed.

"It works!" I shout, not able to contain my elation.

Papa and Uncle congratulate me, but it's premature. Footprints begin to emerge everywhere. The Governor is right, there are too many prints to track. I'm sick inside. I should know by now that every time I try something new, I am disappointed.

The Governor suggests that we all return to his office for tea. I am about to admit defeat, when I notice a weird pattern on the floor. I drop to the ground, with Kaya at my side, to get a closer look. I wish now that I hadn't thought about giving up so easily.

"What are you doing, dear child?" the Governor says in a pompous voice.

"Never mind," Papa says. "Keira knows what she's doing. She's the best spy I have ever worked with."

I notice something different about one of the footprints. I have an exhilarating feeling, a light tickle on the back of the neck that travels to my heels. Perhaps this is the clue I need. I crawl along the floor, following the unusual prints that have emerged under the wax. When I reach the end of the ten-foot area, I repeat the process. Papa, the Commissioner and the Governor stay close behind.

It is slow going. There are hundreds of prints. It's like a 1,000 piece jigsaw puzzle where all the pieces look the same. But hey, Papa says I am a champion at problem-solving. Then suddenly all the prints overlap and it is impossible to track. I twist my magic hat back and forth hoping for a solution. Nothing! I look up at Papa. He sees in my eyes the look of determination not disappointment. I see in his eyes that he is proud of me.

"Keira, what is it that is so special about the prints you are tracking?" Papa asks.

"There appears to be what looks like a spot of blood six inches to the right of one of the foot prints," I say. "Perhaps the thief cut himself on the Sceptre. Let's keep looking."

"Good point. Spread out," Papa says. "Maybe we can find where the footprint and blood spot start again."

Papa and the Commissioner drop to their knees to help. I was glad I had extra sponges. Papa and Uncle Commish begin spreading the solution on different sections of the floor. Waffles remains content in Uncle Commish's arms as Uncle Commish applies the solution to a section of the floor. The Governor's bad leg prevents him from joining in.

Thirty minutes later and still we have not found the prints. Tick-tock, tick-tock, time goes by—my determination doesn't. Another thirty minutes pass, tick-tock, tick-tock. I fight hard not to feel defeated.

"Over here! Over here!" shouts Papa.

The Jewels

Papa and the Commissioner rise slowly from the floor. I can hear their bones crack as they get up in stages. This is followed by ooh's and ah's as they stretch out their stiff muscles.

"Thank you," I say, hoping that will somehow help the pain.

"You are most welcome," they say in unison.

Uncle Commish is still clinging to Waffles. I can't help but notice his cheeriness as he pets him gently. As for Waffles, I've never seen him stay still for this long.

I continue to follow new tracks as time keeps marching along: tick-tock, tick-tock. I approach the red silk rope that blocks tourists from getting too close to the paintings and display cabinets. All the prints end there. I pound my fist on the slate floor. "No, no, no!" I exclaim. I fidget with my magic hat. Again, nothing!

Waffles leaps to the ground and sniffs his way

to a spot just inside the silk rope. I walk over to see
what he is growling at.

"You did it, Waffles, you did it! You found the
paired footprint and blood spot," I announce.

"Well done, Waffles," Uncle Commish adds.

I follow the prints to a wall where they stop. I
look up. Hanging above me is a large portrait of the
Queen. She looks down at me with a smile. Perhaps
she thinks I'm on the right track. The Governor
thinks otherwise.

The Queen

"Dead end," the Governor snickers. "Little girl, you have led us on a wild goose chase. This has been a waste of everyone's valuable time."

The Commissioner, annoyed by the Governor's nasty comment, says, "Let me remind you, Governor, that you are the senior person responsible for the Crown Jewels and their safety. You had better look at yourself if you want to blame someone!"

"I do take responsibility for what happened," the Governor replies. "But I am not the one who put his trust in a girl with a doll to find them."

At the mention of the word *doll*, Papa and the Commissioner know exactly what I will do next. They look down at Kaya.

The Governor ignores his colleague's rebuke, watching me with amusement, thinking that my fidgeting with my doll is playing like any other child would play. Papa and the Commissioner know otherwise. They know that I am about to use my invention.

I rise from the floor and stand between Papa and the Commissioner. I look up at the Queen and curtsy. "Your Majesty," I say, "I want you to meet Kaya. She is about to find your Crown Jewels." I help my doll with her curtsy. Then I raise both of her arms above her head. A loud hum is heard; the application is activated.

I direct the red beam from Kaya's eyes onto the supposedly dead-end wall. Kaya is programmed to identify structural anomalies. My excitement grows as she interprets the signals sputtering back from the wall.

"There is something hidden behind the wall," I announce. The Governor's pompous smirk begins to disappear.

I gently twist Kaya's head to the right. There is a sudden click followed by a rumbling of tumblers behind the portrait of the Queen. The Governor shifts his weight in favor of his stronger foot. His confident smirk seems to have evaporated. His eyes are focused on the Queen. I turn to the Governor and say, "Not to worry, the rumbling you hear is not the Queen's indigestion." Uncle Commish smiles.

We all step back as Her Majesty rotates into the wall. "Oh my, I don't believe it," the Commissioner says, totally astonished.

The Crown Jewels are beautiful.

The Rosebush

"**B**ravo," says Uncle Commish.

"You are amazing," Papa says, picking me up in his arms.

"What about Kaya," I say to Papa. "Doesn't she deserve a kiss, too?"

Papa is sometimes very silly. He turns to Kaya, bows, and then smothers her with kisses. We all laugh, except for the Governor.

Papa hoists me up onto his shoulders and parades me around like a Queen riding on one of her royal Thoroughbred horses. Then he picks up speed for fun, pretending that we are racing at Astor. The finishing line is where the Crown Jewels now rest. The diamonds sparkle on me as we pass. As we do I turn my ahead away, they are too bright for my eyes. For sure, they are priceless.

"The Queen will be so pleased," Commissioner Lamb announces. "Even if we don't know who stole them."

"But we do!" I exclaim. "It was the Governor of the Tower of London himself."

Everyone's jaw falls open, astonished by the accusation. While the Commissioner has confidence in me as a young sleuth, he doesn't agree. "Keira," he says, "the Governor comes from an old, well-established family. His own father had received numerous medals in recognition for his accomplishments as an Ambassador. The Governor himself went to all the best schools and has served his country with great integrity. He could not have done such a thing."

Sensing an opportunity to sway the tide, the Governor says, "Thank you, Commissioner. I have given my life to my country. I am quite offended by this child's accusations. I am even more offended that you and her grandfather have even allowed her involvement."

Papa, on the other hand, trusts my judgment. "Keira, why don't you explain to the Commissioner how you came to this conclusion?"

I smile up at Uncle Commish. "All the beautiful things you say about the Governor are true. But remember, you can hide a lot of rubbish behind a rosebush."

I bring over the chair that had been vacated by the security guard. "Uncle Commish, if you ask the Governor to take a seat, I will demonstrate."

"This is nonsense," the Governor exclaims.

"Please sit," the Commissioner instructs.

Reluctantly the Governor sits, saying as he does, "The Queen will hear about this!"

I kneel down to remove the Governor's right shoe.

"Excuse me, what do you think you are doing? Get your hands off me!" He pushes me away with his foot.

"Ouch! That hurt," I shout. Waffles growls.

"That's enough, Governor Foster," the Commissioner intercedes. "You have a choice. You can do as Keira has asked, or I will order a couple of Beefeaters to come and remove your shoes."

"No need, I am quite capable of doing it myself," the Governor says.

Reluctantly, he presents me his shoe. Anger has now washed away any shyness I might have had. I stand in front of him with his shoe in my left hand looking down at him in the chair.

I stretch out my right hand toward him. "And the cane, dear Governor. I should like to have your cane," I say with an English accent.

I kneel back down on the floor and carefully position his shoe on one of the footprints that led me to the portrait of Her Majesty. I then do the same with the cane. It wasn't a blood spot; it was the bottom of the Governor's cane. A perfect fit, they match the paired prints. *The Case of the Missing Crown Jewels* is solved.

I wonder if Papa is thinking the same thing I am: How could the Governor betray the Queen? How could he betray the people of England?

The Commissioner is stunned. "The Governor steeling the jewels? I never would have suspected that someone of your position would stoop so low as to put your own greed ahead of the welfare of our country," he says in disappointment.

The room goes silent, and then the three of us turn toward the Governor at once.

"It wasn't greed," says the Governor in a tone more like grief, than guilt. He collapses into the chair.

Keira senses there is more to his story; tears are now flowing down his cheeks.

In an almost inaudible voice, he adds, "It wasn't greed that compelled me to do this, it was the safety of my wife. She's been kidnapped. The ransom is the Crown Jewels."

The Letter

Our mouths fall open at the same time; none of us saw this coming. Our eyes reconnect. "Perhaps, Governor, you should explain," the Commissioner gently suggests. Silence again fills the air. The Governor is resting his head on his cane, all energy drained, the emotion taking its toll. Finally, he lifts his head slowly, his eyes puffed by distress. His voice stutters a little as he begins to explain.

"When I came home from work last Friday," the Governor says in an anxious voice, "I was surprised to find that my wife, Katherine, was not at home. We were supposed to drive up to Eton to visit our children. That is the boarding school they attend." His voice cracks at the mention of his children. He looks embarrassed by this unexpected show of emotion. He stiffens slightly and continues.

"I immediately went to the phone to see if she had left a message that she would be late. She hadn't. There was, however, an envelope sitting next to the phone. Printed on the outside of the envelope was, 'Urgent. Open now. Your wife's life depends on it'." He pauses to compose himself, maintaining the English tradition of a *stiff upper lip*.

The Governor continues to explain. "I ripped open the envelope. Inside were specific instructions, including where to hide the jewels, which you have already discovered, thanks to Keira."

The Governor turns to me and says, "I do hope you will accept my apology. You are, as your grandfather has repeated many times, amazing." He then bows. He seems almost relieved that he was caught. The stress of both events, losing his wife and steeling the Crown Jewels, was a burden that was crushing him.

I feel bad that I had misjudged this man. Sure he was the thief, and for that I was right. But I assumed that because he was so stiff and proper, he wasn't caring. It turns out that the Governor is as loving as my own dad. He just shows it in a different way.

"I accept your apology," I say looking him straight in the eyes. "Now let's go find your wife."

"We need to look at the ransom note. That's the only clue we have. I know it's not much, but that's our only hope," says Papa.

We return to the Governor's office. He unlocks his desk drawer and hands Papa the letter the kidnapper had left. Suddenly Waffles leaps out of Uncle Commish's arms and grabs the letter from Papa's hand.

"Waffles, stop!" I shout in a stern voice. "You bring that back right this minute."

Waffles is under the desk sniffing the letter as hard as he can. For some reason he thinks it's food. Papa keeps pretzels in his pocket for such an emergency. Waffles drops the paper in exchange for two pretzels. He's a tough negotiator.

Papa hands the letter to the Commissioner. He reads it then says, "The instructions are as the Governor said. They are specific as to which of the Crown Jewels are wanted, where the Jewels are to be hidden and by when." That was the part that got our attention. We now know that we have only three hours to find the kidnapper.

"I'll never see my wife again," the Governor declares. "I've been such a fool. I should have called you in the beginning, Commissioner. Now I've lost her forever."

"We'll do our best," the Commissioner says, "I will put all our best people on the case immediately."

I am curious as to why Waffles was interested in the ransom note. It's not like him to eat paper. I rotate the note to see if there is a hidden message. There isn't. I look carefully for clues of any kind but I don't see any. I do however notice a hint of a familiar odor. One that drives Waffles crazy.

"I don't think that will be necessary," I say as I stare down at the ransom letter.

"I'm sorry, Keira," Papa says, "please repeat what you said. I don't think the Commissioner heard you."

"Uncle Commish, I don't think you will need to call in your best people," I repeat. "I had a chance to look at the kidnapper's letter. I wanted to find out what it was about the letter that got Waffles so excited." They all turned and looked at me.

"It smells like chocolate."

The Trap

We make our plan. The trap is set.

Commissioner Lamb, Papa and I stop by Director Shallow's office, as we are about to leave. They don't want him to suspect that they know he is the kidnapper.

"Congratulations, Director Shallow," the Commissioner says. "Mr. Jones has given us an A+ for our security. We are lucky to have you in charge."

"Thank you," he says. "I do my best. Would you like a piece of chocolate?"

"Maybe later," Papa says as they shake hands goodbye. They have been careful not to let him suspect that they know he is the kidnapper.

We leave the Tower of London as if all is normal. Director Shallow is unaware that we have found the secret hiding place and that we know it was the Governor who had taken the Crown Jewels and why. He also doesn't know that I hid my doll, Kaya, under a chair near where the jewels are concealed. Her webcam is activated.

We drive to the police station a few blocks away. The Governor is placed in a cell. I promise him that I will find his wife and return her safely. That's my priority. Papa and I enter a small conference room. I turn on Papa's laptop and connect it to Kaya's webcam. All is quiet.

The Commissioner is in the conference room next door, briefing several of his best agents. Shortly thereafter, the agents leave to take their positions outside the Tower.

Commissioner Lamb, Papa and I gather around the laptop, watching, listening, waiting. Waffles is under the conference table sleeping off his reward of pretzels.

The three hours are almost up when we see the first sign of activity inside the vault where the jewels are hidden. The red light on the Tower's security cameras goes off. The Director is making his move.

"The Director has deactivated the alarms," the Commissioner announces, advising his agents that it's almost time to move in.

We hear heavy footsteps, and then strained, winded breathing. Before we even see Director

Shallow, we know it is he that is entering the area. He stands in front of the picture of the Queen.

"He should have bowed," I said.

"Brilliant," Uncle Commish chuckles.

The Director is holding a device that looks like a TV remote. He points it toward the picture, presses a button and the hidden cabinet opens. He freezes.

"That can't be!" the Director shouts. "Where did they go? Where are the Crown Jewels?"

He reaches into the safe and pulls out a box. "Oh no!" he shouts in a panicky voice.

"It's over! They know it's me." He collapses on the floor below the picture of the Queen. His skin covering his heavy frame folds as he slides down the wall. His breathing is loud and uneven. He is too confused to notice Kaya facing him from under the chair. We watch him as he opens the box that was in the safe and takes two pieces of his favorite chocolate.

Caught

The Crown

We are to stop at Buckingham Palace on our way back to the plane. The Queen wants to thank us for solving the case.

Papa's cell phone wakes me from a daydream. "You are welcome. I'll pass the phone to Keira. She'll want to hear it direct from you," he says.

"Hello, who is this?" I ask.

"This is Governor Foster. My wife is here with me and in good health. The Director confessed all, once he was in custody. Katherine was locked in an abandoned warehouse. She'll be fine—we'll be fine, thanks to you. I wish you a safe trip home. Goodbye."

He hangs up before I can ask any questions. I wonder what will happen to him ... I do hope they are lenient. The Governor would never have done what he did if his wife's life hadn't been threatened.

Sir Hazledine is waiting at the Palace steps when we arrive. He opens my door and extends a white-gloved hand to help me out of the car. I smile and curtsy.

"Well done, old girl, well done," he says.

What! Old girl? "Mr. Secretary," I say, in my most serious voice, "I'm only twelve."

This time, with the look of a pleased school-teacher, he says, "In age only, my dear."

I whisper to Kaya, "He definitely likes riddles."

"Keira," Secretary Hazledine says in a warm voice, "I want you to know that if I had ever had a child, I would have wanted her to be exactly like you."

"Oh, I'm so happy that you like me," I say as I hug him. "I like you too, Uncle Secretary."

Suddenly the front door of the Palace opens and a red carpet unrolls down the steps. Soldiers dressed in red with large black fluffy hats march out and line both sides of the carpet. They lift their royal trumpets to their lips and inhale in unison, then blow into their horns, like they do in Cinderella. Sir Hazledine offers me his right arm and we walk together up the red-carpeted steps.

"Follow my lead," he advises.

"What's going on?" I say.

"Shush, do what I do," he says.

Standing at the end of the carpet is the Queen. Splendidly dressed Dukes and Duchesses stand on either side of Her Majesty. Young girls dressed in white are also present. Everyone is looking at me. I hadn't changed from the outfit I was wearing, so I assume it's my peacock fashion that draws their eyes to me. I start to lower my head as shyness sneaks in, but Sir Hazledine clears his throat, signaling me to cut it out.

Papa says, "You're doing great."

I have no idea what he is talking about. I am having a hard time keeping up. Waffles is pulling me toward the Lab, now wanting to be his friend, my hat is slipping off my head and I am losing my grip on Kaya. With a few steps remaining, I drop everything. Waffles takes off toward Horace. My hat and Kaya fall to the floor. Somehow I am able to ignore it all.

I curtsy as I approach the Queen. The Queen nods.

"Keira, you are truly an exceptional young girl. Without your help, we may never have found the Crown Jewels and saved the Governor's wife. With the power bestowed upon me, I award you The Royal Victorian Order, in recognition of your loyalty and good deeds."

The Royal Victorian Order

The trumpets salute me as I step forward and kneel before Her Majesty. She places a blue ribbon, from which the medal hangs, over my head.

"Keira," she declares, "you are the youngest Grand Dame in the history of our country." Everyone applauds and the young girls toss rose petals over me as I rise from my kneeling position.

"Keira," the Queen continues, "I also have something unofficial to give you. You see, when I was your age, I too, was shy. It wasn't until I was crowned a princess that my shyness vanished. This is that very crown. Please kneel, young Keira." I do as she requests. "May this crown," she continues, "be your friend and a reminder of the goodness everyone sees in you." The trumpets blow and more rose petals follow, as does the applause.

"Finally," the Queen says, "I would like you both to be my guest at the Palace for the week."

"I'm afraid we will have to decline, Your Majesty," Papa says. "I promised Keira's mom I would have her home in time for school tomorrow." He turns toward me to look me directly in the eyes.

"Keira, I hope you understand," he says as he rubs his thumb and index finger together.

I nod, confirming I understand the secret message—The Keira and Papa Detective Agency has another case.

Epilogue

The jet engines are running when we arrive at the airport. Waffles jumps over me as I open the car door.

"Be careful of my crown," I warn him.

His tail spins. He barks with crazy enthusiasm running back and forth from the car to the plane. Waffles wants me to follow him. I do. I now see why he is so excited. It is official. The Keira and Papa Detective Agency plane that was provided by the CIA has been renamed *The Flying Waffles*.

"Papa, when did you find the time to have the name of the plane changed?" I ask.

"I didn't," Papa responds.

"I confess," says Uncle Commish. "Waffles was so upset that you named the plane after a Labrador Retriever, I felt compelled to make it right."

Waffles leaps into Uncle Commish's outstretched hands and gives him a good licking. "You're a good boy, and I'm so glad the renaming of the plane has made you happy," he says.

Waffles isn't the only one that's happy. I couldn't help but notice, that every time Uncle Commish is with Waffles, Uncle Commish's sadness disappears into Waffles' fur.

"Uncle Commish, I'll always remember how much I appreciated your kindness when you gave me Kaya." I say. "It was such a surprise. Kaya has been one of those gifts that keeps on giving."

"It was nothing. Heck, that's what friends do," Uncle Commish says.

"Exactly," I respond. "Wait here." I dash up the steps to the plane two at a time. Co-pilot Dick Lasus is waiting for me, holding what I hope will be a big surprise for Uncle Commish.

"Thank you, Dick. I don't know how you did it, but he looks just like Waffles."

"I wish I could take the credit, but it was Sir Hazledine and the Queen herself that made the arrangements. Without them it never would have happened," Dick says.

"Funny, they never said a word to me," I respond, surprised that they didn't want to take credit for such a nice deed.

"Keira, the English take great pride in being humble," Dick says. "It's a wonderful characteristic, don't you think?"

"I think so," I say. I'm not really sure. I like to get credit when I do something nice. On the other hand, the idea of just letting the recognition surface without bragging makes the deed more genuine and sincere. I'll have to discuss this with Papa when I get a chance. Now that I think about it, Papa is like that too.

Uncle Commish sees me first as I make my way down the steps. His ultra-serious face is now brighter than the Queen's diamond studded Royal Crown.

"Uncle Commish, this is my special present for you," I announce in a tone mixed with pride and a touch of giggle. "I do hope that you like him."

He bows and says, "You are indeed a very special child." His voice cracks. He pauses to regain control of his emotion. "Let me rephrase that. You are indeed a very special friend. Not only are you an amazing spy, but also you have to be the kindest person I have ever known. Thank you, Keira. He's perfect."

"How and when did you do this?" Papa asks. "He even looks exactly like Waffles."

"I have some special friends that made it happen. I think they would prefer to remain anonymous. They're the ones that really deserve the credit," I say. Hmmm, that felt good.

"Uncle Commish, what do you think you will name him?" I ask.

"That's an easy one. Bacon might be appropriate, don't you think?" he announces.

Our cheers and laughter confirm his choice. Waffles on the other hand is totally confused. All at once he sees what appears to be his reflection, Bacon, and hears the announcement that his favorite food might be arriving—bacon. His tail starts spinning, his nose starts sniffing and his tongue flaps out the side of his mouth.

I take Waffles from the Commissioner's arms in exchange for Bacon. He is rewarded with puppy licks and lots of wiggles of joy. The Commissioner responds with a face-snuggle into his fur. He holds Bacon's face in his hands, puts his own face just inches from Bacon and says, "Do you think you would like to be the assistant commissioner of Scotland Yard?"

"Ruff, ruff," Bacon responds. We all applaud.

"I hate to break up the fun, but I'm afraid we really must leave," Papa declares.

I hug Uncle Commish goodbye. Our tears meet as they drop to the ground. Waffles manages to reach over far enough to give Uncle Commish one final lick. "You're a great friend, too, Waffles. You don't realize it, but your crazy antics, and generous lickings have relit my spirit. Thank you," he says as he ruffles Waffles head.

"Now Bacon," I say, "you take good care of Uncle Commish." Waffles barks as if confirming my instructions.

I race up the steps to the plane. Papa is calling. My emotions are also in conflict. All the joy, celebration, and happiness is somewhat depleted by our goodbyes and pending departure.

mn

Our jet levels off at 45,000 feet.

"Keira, I believe your thoughtful gift to the Commissioner is an extraordinary act of kindness," Papa says. "How did you know that he would even want a dog?"

"Papa, did you not see how often Uncle Commish asked to hold Waffles and how he lit up with happiness every time he did?" I ask. "For a spy, you miss some obvious things," I chuckle.

"Thank goodness I have 'Little Miss Eagle Eye' to cover for me," he laughs.

"All kidding aside, Keira, I have enjoyed working with you, solving this case," Papa says.

"I know," I say. "Being back in the spy business is giving you the excitement and adventure you need to be happy."

"Initially I thought that too," Papa says. "But sharing an experience with you is what I liked most. We could have been playing miniature golf and I would have enjoyed it as much. What I am saying is that being a spy is fun, but being your grandfather is the best."

The phone rings. Papa takes the call. It's the Commissioner.

"Aha! Interesting. Aha! I understand. Thanks for the info." He hangs up.

"Papa, what did Uncle Commish tell you that so surprised you?" I ask.

Papa explains. "Director Shallow admitted to everything. He will be going to jail for a long time."

"What about the Governor? He was only trying to save his wife," I ask.

"That's true," Papa says. "But what he did was wrong. If not for you, the Crown Jewels might have been lost forever. If that happened, there would be chaos throughout the country. No, the Governor should have gone to the police immediately."

"Will he go to jail?" I ask, hoping that the answer will be no.

"Perhaps," Papa responds. "Just because he has an important position and knows the Queen, he should not be treated differently than anyone else."

"I understand," I answer. "It's just like the teacher's favorite student shouldn't receive a higher grade if it is not earned."

"You got it," Papa says. "However, I do believe that the courts would treat anyone in this situation with leniency. Sometimes good people make poor choices in a split second, thinking they are doing what is best. I feel sure that they will take that into consideration."

"I get it, Papa, and I sure hope you are right."

"Papa, what are you going to tell Grandma and my parents when we show up with Waffles untrained and a day late?" I ask. "They think we're at obedience school."

Papa responds slowly. He seems uncomfortable about something. "I spoke with your mom earlier. I explained that Waffles had run away, that we only just found him and that we would be a day late. She wanted to speak with you but I told her you were asleep. I didn't want to put you in a position where you couldn't tell the truth."

"But why is it OK if you don't tell the truth," I ask.

"When I work with the government, I am sworn to secrecy. If I break that oath it is a federal offense; it is against the law. As a rule, I tell the truth, but in cases like this I can't. These are the contradictions that sometimes leave a bad taste and make you feel bad when you have to lie," he says. "We sometimes call that a 'little white lie.'"

"I understand. I know that sometimes I have to say something to a friend that is misleading because I don't want to hurt his or her feelings," I say, nodding my head.

"Keira," Papa continues, "you know, you answered a lot of questions and found solutions to difficult problems without always using your magic hat. I also noticed that you were not so shy. I'm thinking the best thing about the magic hat is that it gave you confidence to be you—the amazing you I know you are."

"Goodnight, Papa. I love you," I say.

"I love you too, Gumdrop," Papa says, "big time."

Create, solve or discuss your own mystery.

KEIRA and her grandfather, PAPA, developed their special bond by solving a mystery. YOU can too, even without a magic hat. You just need a QUESTION, a grandparent and a library, a bookstore, or a computer to help you investigate the answers. Here are just a few ideas:

Countries have their own mysteries?

- Make up your own mystery to solve with a question like, *"What kind of animals do they have in Saudi Arabia, and why? In India, how do people know everything about a person just by his or her name? Which country only allows parents to have one child, and why?"*

How do robots work?

- *You and your grandparent can learn how to build one. It's not as hard as it sounds.*

Why do dogs, like Waffles, have better noses than humans?

Why do birds that live in Maine in the summer go to Florida in the winter?

Sometimes it's fun to ask QUESTIONS about a book you and your grandparent are reading. OR you could even create your OWN MYSTERY. Just START with the best question of all: WHAT IF...? And see what happens.

- *Maybe you can work together to come up with a different ending.*

- *Gather your friends together with a grandparent to write a short mystery. The grandparent can begin by explaining the crime that was committed. Then go in a circle with each participant adding to the story. You will enjoy how much fun your friends have sharing time with your grandparent.*

- *Write a short mystery (it could be as short as three pages) with a grandparent, with each of you as a lead character. Then act it out for the family.*

Sometimes you may have QUESTIONS about the mysteries of your own life, about friends or school that are confusing, maybe hard to talk about with a parent. KEIRA and her PAPA talked a lot and learned to trust each other. All you need to do is ASK the right QUESTION. Here are some examples of everyday life mysteries you might DISCUSS with a grandparent:

- *Why is a certain classmate so mean?*

- *Why does my brother or sister act this way?*

- *What's so important about music lessons?*

- *Why doesn't my friend like me anymore?*

- *Why does my mom yell at my dad sometimes?*

- *Why do I feel sad or not good enough?*

- *Why do I have to shake hands with people I am introduced to?*

- *Ask your grandparent to show you a picture of your mom or dad when they were your age. Let your grandparent explain a situation that bothered your parent back then. Then discuss ways in which you could have gained a good understanding so that you could provide advice. You will need to ask a lot of questions to solve this mystery.*

Visit my website for more:
RobertMartinAuthor.com

Coming Soon from

The Keira and Papa Detective Agency

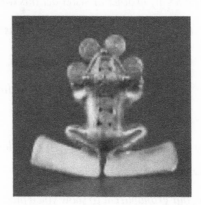

The Case of
the Golden Key

Robert Martin
with Keira Martin Ely

Prologue

The plane pounds hard onto the runway. It startles me awake. We're home. I'm still wearing the medallion the Queen of England presented to me. I saved a life, prevented the country from chaos and helped solve *The Case of the Missing Crown Jewels*. My name is Keira. I'm 12. I'm a spy. I wish I could tell my parents.

The U.S. Government has an agency that spies on foreign governments, organizations and individuals. It's called the Central Intelligence Agency or CIA. In addition to collecting and analyzing intelligence, they carry out covert activities. These activities are conducted by its own employees, the U.S. military or by other partners. The Keira and Papa Detective Agency is one of the "other partners." That's whom I work for. I'm the only kid in its worldwide network of spies.

Papa is my grandfather. He has always been a spy. He recruited me when I found a magic hat that gives me special powers to invent crime fighting devices and to quickly access information. Kaya, my American Girl Doll, is equipped with some of my inventions. Together we solve mysteries before they can cause havoc in a country or destroy the world.

"Where are we going, Papa?" I ask. "We're already a day late. Why aren't we going to my home in Brooklyn? Why are we heading toward your house?"

"It's a surprise," he says.

Waffles' ears perk up. "Surprise" means treats in dog language. His tail begins to pound. Waffles is my misbehaving dog. He has a good nose for crime, not to mention food.

"Now, don't ask any more questions," Papa continues.

Papa sees me looking out the window as I tell him how beautiful the changing colors of the fall leaves are: "I just love the different shades of red, brown, green and yellow, and how they all come together just to please our eyes like Grandma does with the different ingredients in brownies that please our taste."

Papa asks, "Do you know why the leaves change colors?"

"Of course I do," I respond as I put my magic hat on. This allows me to get the information I want in seconds. "Leaves contain a chemical called chlorophyll, which makes them green. When the sun shines longer and there is lots of light through-out the day, there is more of the chemical chlorophyll and the leaves are very green. When there is less sun, like in the fall, there is less chlorophyll and therefore less green. That is when the other color pigments start to show, leaves change colors, and eventually drop to the ground."

"Amazing" he says, as we pull into the Darien police station in Connecticut.

Waffles jumps to the floor and hides his face under his two front paws. The dog pound is in the back of the station. That's where they put misbehaving dogs that escape from their owners. He's been here before.

There is a woman in a military uniform—a Marine—waiting at the station's entrance. She stands very straight. Her uniform is blue with lots of badges and stripes. The sword at her side is very cool. She salutes us like a soldier in the *Nutcracker Suite*. She opens my door and says: "Good morning, Miss Keira." What! How come she knows my name? Why are we at a police station? What is Papa up to this time? Waffles scrunches up into a ball thinking the soldier won't be able to see him. I say goodbye to Waffles as I slam the door shut. He looks up at me annoyed that I gave his hiding place away. Papa parks the car, leaving the window open. He knows Waffles won't jump out and venture anywhere near the pound.

The lady Marine guard rushes us up two flights of stairs. I keep my head down as I walk past the smiling policemen's stares. I avoid their welcoming smiles. I feel very uncomfortable among strangers. I'd rather avoid people than meet them. There are also other marine guards stationed along the stairs. It feels like I've entered another world—why all these policemen and why so many marine soldiers?

As we continue down the corridor, I keep looking for jail cells hoping to see a bad guy but there are none.

"Papa, why does Darien have such a large police station if there are no bad guys to put in it?" I ask.

Papa says, "How did you figure that out? You're pretty smart even without your magic hat."

"What! Papa, what has that got to do with my question?"

"You'll see when you get older."

I hate it when grown-ups say that.

We enter a conference room in the back of the building. I see my surprise. Standing in her well-decorated uniform is my special friend General Marco. She coached me early on, during my spy training at Langley, the headquarters for the CIA.

"Thank you, Papa. This is the best surprise ever," I shout, as I give her a big hug.

"What are you doing here?" I ask in a tone that captures my excitement.

Before she can respond the building starts to shake. The noise is like a steady stream of thunder. I am trying not to show fear. A glass of water falls from the table and shatters. The pictures on the walls sway back and forth.

Then suddenly, all is calm again.

"Papa, what was that? Was that an earthquake?"

"No," he responds. "That was a ..." and before he can finish, a door slams open from the roof above and stomping feet start heading our way.

"Papa," I yell. "These must be the bad guys. This is why the police station is so big. The bad guys are coming after us."

"Keira, everything is alright. These are not bad guys. In fact this is your surprise," Papa announces.

"Wait a minute," I say. "I thought General Marco was my surprise. Nothing can beat that."

General Marco says, "Keira there is someone here who wants to meet you." She opens the conference room door. "Keira," she continues, "say hello to the President of the United States of America. "

It was the President's helicopter that made the building vibrate and the deafening noise. Wow, the President, the first woman President, coming to see me! I wish my mom and dad were here. They speak of her often. They like that President Tapella is an independent, former CEO, former Governor, lived overseas for ten years and is fluent in three languages. As for me, I like her smile. The fact that she is a woman makes me wonder why there aren't more women in senior leadership positions.

"How are you?" says the President.

Shyly, I say, "OK," but I don't think she hears me. I am not sure what to do. I've never hung out with a President before.

"I have heard so much about you," she says.

My shoulders slump; I am embarrassed by all the attention. Her kind smile relaxes me a little.

The President then says, "Keira, our nation thanks you for the help you provided Commissioner Lamb in solving *The Case of the Missing Crown Jewels*." She explains that without my help, they never would have recovered the Crown Jewels and saved the life of the wife of the Governor of the Tower of London. At which point the President bends down and places the Congressional Medal around my neck. "You are the youngest recipient ever. Congratulations."

The excitement is too much. I don't faint, but I zone out. Nothing makes sense. I open my eyes and glance around the room. Nothing changed except that Papa's smile is a lot wider.

I then whisper in Papa's ear if it would be OK to hug the President of the United States ... and I do. I'm not always shy.

The Call

It's a rainy, dreary summer day. It is 5:30 A.M. and I'm up. My mom, dad and sister are not. Papa is. I just received his text message. An old friend of his, Ricardo Martinelli, who is now the President of Panama, has contacted him. His government must find a hidden treasure of gold before a band of corrupt soldiers from Nicaragua do. The Keira and Papa Detective Agency has another case. And I thought this was going to be a boring day.

"Hi Papa," I say as I kiss him on the cheek. Kaya, my American Girl Doll, does the same.

"And good morning to you too Gumdrop," he replies and ruffles my red hair. Gumdrop is the nickname he gave me. His way of letting me know he thinks I'm special. I have to say it works.

"Papa!" I say, holding Kaya for him to see.

"And a big time good morning to you, Kaya," he says bending over to kiss her cheek. "Hey, where's Waffles?"

I explain that Waffles stopped to visit a fire hydrant. Then we see him coming around the corner at full speed. Papa opens his door just in time for Waffles to leap straight up into his arms. Papa pretends not to like the face washing he is receiving. "Stop it Waffles," he chuckles. I don't think he is trying very hard to get Waffles to stop.

The team is back together: Papa, me, Kaya and Waffles; The Keira and Papa Detective Agency is back on assignment.

"What did you tell your parents?" Papa inquires. My parents still don't know that Papa and I are spies.

"They're not up yet. I left a note saying that we're off on a new adventure and that I will call them later," I tell him.

"Perfect," he says.

My parents have come to expect Papa to arrive unannounced to go on an adventure with me. Last month we went hot air ballooning in the Berkshires. It was scary but a thrill I enjoyed.

"Where are we headed?" I ask.

"Crown Heights, which is sometimes referred to as 'Little Panama,'" he says. "It's only two and a half miles from here. That's where El Gordo lives."

El Gordo means big in Spanish, which he is. Real big! His actual name is Carlos Ortega. El

Gordo is from Panama. He had worked for Papa there and was instrumental in the capture of the ruthless General Noriega. Now he works for the head of the CIA, General Patti Marco. Waffles and I like him a lot.

We arrive at his modest home in ten minutes. His home is painted in cheerful colors like many of the homes in Panama. The streets are quiet. It's Sunday. It's raining harder now. Papa rings the doorbell but no one inside hears it. The pounding rain on the house's tin roof is too much competition for the gentle ring of the chimes.

"Now what?" I ask.

"Perhaps Waffles can help," Papa says. "El Gordo always sleeps with the window open."

Although Waffles hates the rain, he loves the spicy treats El Gordo feeds him when no one is looking. Papa opens the car door for Waffles to leave the car. He doesn't budge.

"Here Waffles," I call. Still nothing.

"El Gordo has a treat," Papa yells.

Waffles bolts out of the car, scoots around the corner of the house slipping and sliding through the mud, and then leaps through the open window landing directly on El Gordo's face.

El Gordo is now drenched and coated in mud. Some adults would be very angry, but not El Gordo.

"Waffles! Buenos días (good morning) my little friend," he shouts with a hearty laugh. "OK, OK, *ya voy, ya voy* (I'm coming, I'm coming)," he says as Waffles pulls him toward the kitchen. Waffles knows where every kitchen is in every house he has ever been in.

Finally the front door opens and we are welcomed with a giant smile and warm *abrazos* (a hug with a couple of pats on the back).

"I hope we didn't wake Sonya," Papa says.

"She's in Panama visiting her mother. I plan to fly down next week," El Gordo says.

"I think you should plan for tomorrow instead. We have another case," Papa says, and then tells him about President Martinelli's call and the hidden treasure.

"Jefe (boss), these are very dangerous people. For them, power and money are more important than lives and family," explains El Gordo, just as a rock comes crashing through the window. There is a note on it, "Come to Panama and you will never leave."

Acknowledgments

The gifted authors who have instructed and mentored me: Kim Barnes (KimBarnes.com), Emma Walton Hamilton (EmmaWaltonHamilton.com), Mary Karr (MaryKarr.com), Peter Lerangis (PeterLerangis.com), Robert Reeves, Roger Rosenblatt, Heather Sellers (HeatherSellers.com), and Gail Sheehy (GailSheehy.com).

Writers who have provided inspiration and advise: Ruth Bonapace, Francine Moyer, Peter Nelson and the too many to mention; SCBWI conference authors, illustrators, agents, publishers and editors.

Close friends who encouraged and provided input (too many to name individually): friends at Fiddlesticks CC in Fort Myers, FL.; friends at the Wee Burn CC in Darien, CT.; and my good buddies from the Aspectuck days.

The dynamic artistic team: Judith Briles (TheBook Shepherd.com), Nick Zelinger (NZGraphics.com), and Tracy Rudd.

My daughters, Tricia and Colette, for their many suggestions and enthusiastic encouragement.

Pam, my high school sweetheart and spouse for almost 50 years, whose ongoing support and insight made the writing journey more than just a book.

Email Robert Martin if you want to be notified when *The Case of the Golden Key* is available.

Bob@RobertMartinAuthor.com

About the Authors

Robert Martin & Keira Martin Ely

Robert Martin is Keira's grandfather and lives with his wife, Pam, in Florida. He is an advocate of building strong family bonds and active in charities for children internationally. His extensive travel to more than 80 countries has shown him that the stress of everyday living is taking its toll on the health of families, particularly children. He believes that grandparents can help—they can be an emotional rock, a wise friend and a playful elder. There is no greater bond than the trust and love between a grandparent and their grandchild.

Robert is a retired division president of a Fortune 100 company and has lived in West Africa, Latin America and Asia. His writing has been published in newspapers and magazines. Robert can be contacted through his website: **RobertMartinAuthor.com**

Keira Martin Ely lives in New York City with her mom, dad, sister and Maggie, her Golden-doodle. She has been writing short stories for her parents since she was six-years old. Keira plays the classical guitar, and loves sports.

Although young herself, she cares deeply about the happiness and welfare of other children. Her sensitivity and keen insight provide her with the ability to relate to a wide array of concerns faced by children. This, and a creative imagination, bring to life each scene, each feeling in her writings.

The Case of the Missing Crown Jewels:

Kids are talking ...

"Keira and her grandfather make a great team together. I liked the way they teased each other and the mutual affection they share."
                                —Cameron

"This is a great book for readers who love mysteries. The ending was a total surprise."
                                —Evan

"I thought this book was super and I could not put it down!"
                                —Dylan

Grandparents are talking ...

"*The Case of the Missing Crown Jewels* describes in an entertaining and provocative fashion, a special relationship between a grandfather and his granddaughter."
                                —Mapes and Charlie Stamm

"A willingness, even an eagerness, to try new things, visit new places and the freedom to let your imagination create fun and solve problems are things every grandpa should encourage in his grandkids."

—Larry Lamattina

"The relationship between Keira and Papa is solidified by the way they work together, their belief in each other. Young and old alike will benefit from reading this story."

—Barbara Lyski

"What a wonderful story for all Grandparents to share with their Grandchildren."

—Barbara Keating

Librarians and teachers are talking ...

"The story promotes using one's imagination and encourages children to take risks. An added feature is it acquaints children with some of the history, customs and practices of another country."

—Judith E. Mosse B.S., M.Ed.

"The author employs a lot of history, countries' traditions, life's lessons, multicultural phrases and great vocabulary."

—Cynthia Brazer, Educator

"The story promotes using one's imagination and encourages children to take risks. An added feature is it acquaints children with some of the history, customs and practices of another country."

—Judith E. Mosse B.S., M.Ed.

"*The Case of the Missing Crown Jewels* does a wonderful job of showing young people the importance of asking good questions."

—Frannie Moyer

"Bravo to Papa and Keira for showing us all how fun the love of learning and adventure really is. These two are quite a treasure."

—Kimberly Spence, Educator

Psychologists are talking ...

"I highly recommend this creative and imaginative book. This book offers an opportunity for family members to deepen the relationship by engaging in reading together and implementing the exercises at the end."

—Rev. Dr. John G. Brown III,
pastoral counselor and psychoanalyst

"This book is a wise and gentle exploration of human nature, told with humor and creativity, wrapped in a story that will capture the imagination of its youthful readers and inspire grandparents who share it with them to enrichment of their relationships with their grandchildren."

—Carol Tolonen, Developmental Psychologist,
educational consultant,
lecturer on education and parenting

"Bob and Keira incorporate into their story the critical developmental topics of self-esteem and character building necessary for emotional success."

—Dr. Audrey Sherman, Psychologist,
Author of *Dysfunction Interrupted*,
Founder of PsychSkills

"The Keira and Papa Detective Agency nurtures the grandparent grandchild bond enabling resilient children. This is a lovely book that celebrates this important relationship and nurtures it further."
—Michelle B. Viro, Ph.D., Licensed Psychologist -
Specialty Children and Families